This book was given to

_____

by

_____

with love

on _____ 19 _____

Honey Bunch

A keepsake storybook of the funny names moms and dads call their babies

Lisa Ann Marsoli & Vickey Bolling

LONGSTREET PRESS, INC.
Atlanta, Georgia

For our own honey bunches,

Emma & Destin,

who inspired this book

while still in our tummies.

Library of Congress Card Catalog Number 95 - 82228

Published by
LONGSTREET PRESS, INC.
A subsidiary of Cox Newspapers,
A subsidiary of Cox Enterprises, Inc.
2140 Newmarket Parkway
Suite 118
Marietta, GA 30067

Produced by Bumpy Slide Books - Los Angeles

ISBN: 1-56352-291-8

Honey Bunch

*A keepsake storybook of the funny names
moms and dads call their babies*

Written by Lisa Ann Marsoli
Illustrated by Vickey Bolling

You are my precious pumpkin,
My cutest cutie pie,

My one and only little lamb,
The apple of my eye.

You are my perfect angel,
My ray of bright sunshine.

*My favorite
jumping jellybean,*

I'm glad that you are mine.

Sometimes you are my love bug,
Sometimes my dear sweet pea,

A munchkin and a honey bunch,
That's what you are to me.

'Cause when I call you silly names,
My special dream come true...

*W*hat I'm really saying is,
Your mommy sure loves you!

Written here are all the names I've made up just for you...

_____

_____

_____

_____

_____

_____

_____

_____

_____

And all of the kooky things your daddy calls you, too.

_____

_____

_____

_____

_____

_____

_____

_____

I love the funny faces that you sometimes make at me...

Tape or glue photo here

They're right here in these pictures,
as you can plainly see!

Tape or glue photo here

Here's a little list of silly words you like to say...

_____

_____

_____

_____

_____

_____

_____

_____

*Together we will read this book,
and laugh at them someday!*

_____

_____

_____

_____

_____

_____

_____

_____